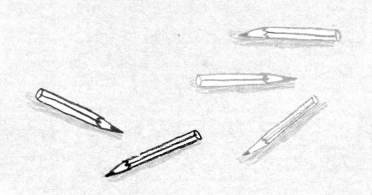

STELLA
Brings the
FAMILY

STELLA
Brings the
FAMILY

by Miriam B. Schiffer

illustrations by Holly Clifton-Brown

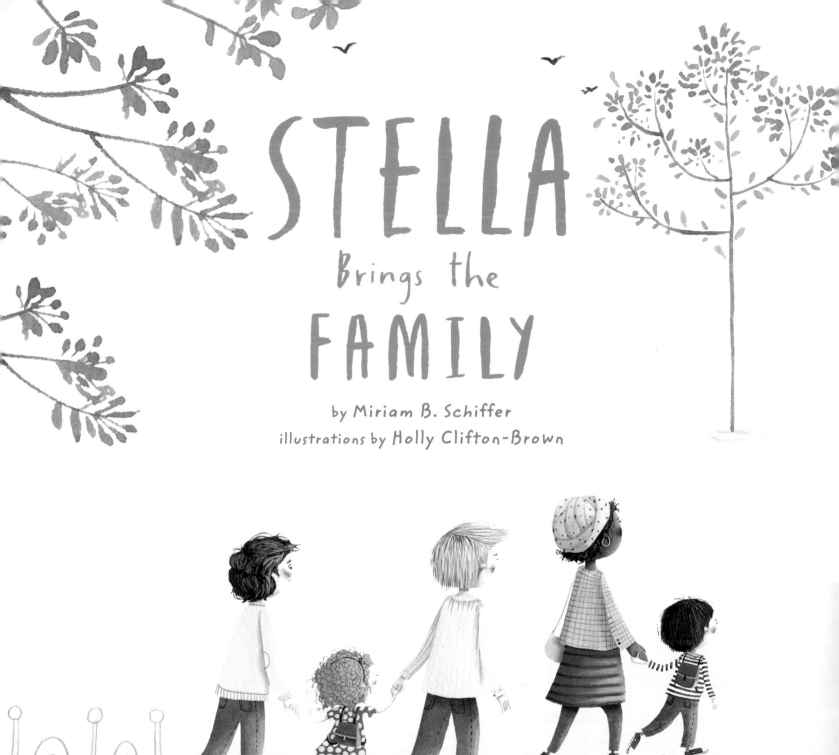

ELMWOOD ELEMENTARY SCHOOL

chronicle books · san francisco

With a hug goodbye . . .

Stella dashed to her cubby and raced to her spot.
Mrs. Abbott had a surprise for the class!

"We're going to have a celebration for Mother's Day," she said, "and each of you can invite a special guest."

Jonathan and Leon said they'd invite their moms. Carmen was sure her mamá would come.

But Stella had two dads.

Everyone else had a mother. Howie had two!

Stella would be the only one without a mother
at the Mother's Day party.

That afternoon, Stella and her clay stared at each other.

The next day, Stella worried about the party when she should have been worrying about other things.

All week, Stella's appetite was gone.

"What's wrong, Stella?" Jonathan asked.

"I have no mother to bring for the Mother's Day celebration."

"No mother?" asked Leon. "But who packs your lunch like my mom does for me?"

"Daddy knows just what I like," said Stella. "The problem isn't lunch. It's that I have no mother to bring for the Mother's Day party."

"*No mother?*" asked Howie. "But who reads you bedtime stories like my mothers do for me?"

"Daddy and Papa read stories to me," said Stella.

"But who kisses you when you are hurt?" Carmen asked.

"Well, that's a long answer," said Stella.

"I get lots of kisses when I'm hurt. Either from Papa or Daddy or Nonna or Aunt Gloria or Uncle Bruno or Cousin Lucy. But I still have no special guest for Mother's Day."

Jonathan asked,
"Why don't you invite them all?"

"What a wonderful idea!"
Papa and Daddy said.

But Stella wasn't so sure.

Soon, the children were crafting invitations, decorating, and preparing gifts.

Stella worked harder than everyone.

The big day arrived! Daddy, Papa, Nonna, Uncle Bruno, Aunt Gloria, and Cousin Lucy went with Stella to school. She had so many guests. Stella hoped it would be okay.

The party was better than Stella had imagined.

Howie came with his two moms, and Jonathan brought his grandmother while his mom was away.

Stella had the biggest crowd of all.

mama Carmen

Mon Leon

They squeezed into the story circle

nonna   daddy Papa   Stella

mommy MOM

Howie

mom Granny
Jonathan

and made frames for their art.

ucy Uncle
bruno aunt
Gloria

Please
Come
to Our
Party

Stella thought the day was turning out fine.
In fact, it was better than fine.

Papa was a big hit.

HAPPY MOTHER'S DAY

Later that day, Mrs. Abbott was worn out.

Stella told her not to worry. For Father's Day, she wouldn't bring nearly as many people.

Just two.

For my mother, Isabel Baker. —M.B.S.

For Danny & Mike. —H.C.B.

Library of Congress Cataloging-in-Publication Data:

Schiffer, Miriam B., author.
Stella brings the family / by Miriam B. Schiffer;
illustrations by Holly Clifton-Brown.
pages cm

Summary: Stella brings her two fathers to school to celebrate Mother's Day.

ISBN 978-1-4521-1190-2 (alk. paper)

1. Gay fathers—Juvenile fiction. 2. Gay parents—Juvenile fiction.
3. Families—Juvenile fiction. 4. Mother's Day—Juvenile fiction.
[1. Gay fathers—Fiction. 2. Gay parents—Fiction. 3. Families—Fiction.
4. Mother's Day—Fiction.] I. Clifton-Brown, Holly, illustrator. II. Title.

PZ7.S34613St 2015
[E]—dc23

2013033259

Manufactured in China.

Design by Nadia Izazi.
Typeset in Zemke Hand ITC and Grenadine MVB.
The illustrations in this book were rendered in watercolor.

10 9 8 7 6 5 4 3

Chronicle Books LLC
680 Second Street
San Francisco, California 94107

Chronicle Books—we see things differently.
Become part of our community at www.chroniclekids.com.